First published 1998 by Walker Books Ltd
87 Vauxhall Walk, London SE11 5HJ

4 6 8 10 9 7 5 3

Text © 1998 Marjorie Newman
Illustrations © 1998 Ben Cort

This book has been typeset in
Bembo Educational.

Printed in Hong Kong

British Library Cataloguing in Publication Data
A catalogue record for this book is available
from the British Library.

ISBN 0-7445-6053-5

To Paul
*M.N.*

To Mum,
Dad and Ruth
*B.C.*

# HORNPIPE'S HUNT FOR PIRATE GOLD

## Marjorie Newman

### illustrated by
### Ben Cort

WALKER BOOKS
AND SUBSIDIARIES

LONDON • BOSTON • SYDNEY

**Under this flap, and the one on page 23, you'll find lots of extra things to spot in the big pictures.**

**When you have finished reading the story, open out the flaps and start searching!**

This is the story of Captain Hornpipe, his pirate crew and a search for hidden gold.

It all began when his enemy, Crossbones Pete, found a treasure map. Pete's ship had sunk, so he plotted to send the map to Captain Hornpipe – who loved treasure hunts – then hide on board **his** ship...

The pirates had quite an adventure and needed to solve a lot of puzzles on the way.

**Can you help Captain Hornpipe?**

- **Read the story and solve the puzzles.**

- **Check your answers at the back when you reach the end, or if you get really stuck.**

Sneakily, Crossbones Pete sent the treasure map to Captain Hornpipe.

Captain Hornpipe guessed Pete was up to no good. But he would look for the treasure anyway.

The trouble was that he couldn't make head or tail of Pete's map.

**Can you help Captain Hornpipe work out where the gold is buried on Grimstone Island?**

TREASURE MAP of GRIMSTONE ISLAND

Start by the two crossed trees.

Find a path between two black rocks.

Go through the trees.

Pass a pond.

Look for the red flowers. We planted them to mark the spot.

To find the gold, you must get there before the flowers die.

Love
Crossbones Pete

Captain Hornpipe rushed to set sail. But some of the sails were ripped! How could the pirates reach the treasure?

Suddenly Captain Hornpipe remembered the ship belonging to his friend Miranda.

He told Sleepy what Miranda's ship looked like. "Run over and ask Miranda if we can borrow it!" he cried.

But Sleepy wasn't listening properly!

**Can you help him find Miranda's ship? It's the one with a green flag, anchored between a red ship and a black ship.**

Miranda said she would lend them her ship — but only if she could come too! She knew Captain Hornpipe would say yes.

Captain Hornpipe told his crew to pack — and to hurry! They would catch a bus to the ship.

Oh dear! Sleepy missed the bus.

**Can you help him catch the next one? It must match the bus that Captain Hornpipe is on.**

Miranda was very excited when they arrived. She didn't notice that Pete had arrived too!

Captain Hornpipe told Untidy to go below and unpack.

Untidy got into an awful muddle!
He, Captain Hornpipe and
Sleepy had each brought five
things. But which chests should
they go in?

**Can you help Untidy?
Match the colours and
patterns of their things to
the labels on the chests.**

They set sail, but Captain Hornpipe couldn't work out which way to go.

Miranda said **she** would work out the route to Grimstone Island.

"I'll keep watch in case Pete is following us," said Captain Hornpipe. He didn't know that Pete had no ship.

But Miranda couldn't find her glasses. Untidy had put them somewhere and there wasn't time to look for them.

**Can you help Miranda pick the best way to go? They mustn't go through whirlpools or past crocodiles.**

GRIMSTONE ISLAND

That evening
they ate a huge supper.

Afterwards, Captain Hornpipe
went off to steer the ship and
keep a look-out for Pete.

Sleepy and Untidy got ready for bed.

Miranda made up some bedtime riddles about things she could see in the cabin.

**Please show Sleepy and Untidy the answers, or they won't be able to sleep tonight!**

What goes "oink" and looks after your money?

What is cuddly, brown and furry?

What is green, feathery and has a red beak?

What is round and has eight legs?

What has wings and ears and hangs upside-down?

Next day the ship sailed fast for Grimstone Island.

They anchored the ship. Then they rowed ashore. Pete watched them all go...

They landed on the island, but couldn't decide which path to take.

**Can you help Captain Hornpipe find a safe, clear path up the cliff to the two crossed trees?**

They found the treasure!

Sleepy and Untidy took the first load back to the ship. But Pete attacked them and tied them up.

**Before Pete fell into the sea ...**

Then Pete went ashore. "I'm having the treasure **and** your ship," he yelled. "And I'm leaving you two behind on the island."

There was a huge fight! Captain Hornpipe fought well, but Miranda finally won the battle with her rugby tackle. Pete went flying into the sea!

 **Can you spot five other things that happened?**

and after.

Captain Hornpipe and Miranda soon rescued Sleepy and Untidy.

And it was Crossbones Pete who was left behind on the island, while the others sailed away.

That night they had a party. Captain Hornpipe wishes you could have been there! But during the party they mislaid some of the treasure (and this time it wasn't Untidy's fault!).

 Can you help them find a pearl necklace, a ring and two gold coins?

 Under this flap, and the one on page 4, you'll find lots of extra things to spot in the big pictures.

 When you have finished reading the story, open out the flaps and start searching!

# The Answers

- The answers to the story puzzles are shown with single black lines.
- The answers to the fun flap puzzles are shown with double black lines.

## Pages 4 and 5

## Pages 6 and 7

## Pages 8 and 9

## Pages 10 and 11

## Pages 12 and 13

## Pages 14 and 15

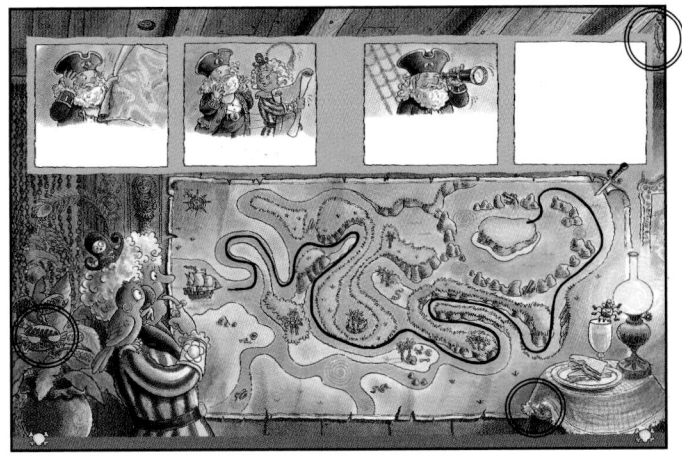

## Pages 16 and 17

## Pages 18 and 19

## Pages 20 and 21

## Pages 22 and 23

# MORE WALKER PAPERBACKS
## For You to Enjoy

Some Skill Level 1 Gamebooks

### GHOST HUNT AT TREMBLY TOWERS

by Molly Williams/Chris Fisher

A hair-raising haunted-house puzzle adventure.

0-7445-6051-9   £4.99

### HORNPIPE'S HUNT FOR PIRATE GOLD

by Marjorie Newman/Ben Cort

A swashbuckling pirate puzzle adventure.

0-7445-6053-5   £4.99

### A BRAVE KNIGHT TO THE RESCUE!

by Stella Maidment/Cathy Gale

A thrilling knight puzzle quest.

0-7445-6055-1   £4.99

### SPACE CHASE ON PLANET ZOG

by Karen King/Alan Rowe

A zappy space puzzle adventure.

0-7445-6050-0   £4.99

### MYSTERY OF THE MONSTER PARTY

by Deri Robins/Anni Axworthy

A monstrous puzzle adventure.

0-7445-6054-3   £4.99

### THE WONDERFUL JOURNEY OF CAMERON CAT

by Marjorie Newman/Charlotte Hard

An entertaining cat puzzle adventure.

0-7445-6052-7   £4.99